My name is Sandy.
I'd like to tell you a story
  about a friend that I met.
It is a special experience that I will
  never forget.

I remember the first day of school.
Summer was gone, time for books
  and class rules.

Meeting new friends is always
  so much fun.
An exciting year had quickly begun.

Victoria's Smile

by Rita Geller
Illustrated by Rita Geller's students

SCHOLASTIC INC.
New York Toronto London Auckland Sydney
Mexico City New Delhi Hong Kong Buenos Aires

Dedicated to my husband, my family, and my friends who encouraged me to continue this project, and to all those individuals with a "special smile," especially Victoria.
—R.G.

I want to express my deep appreciation to the Broward County Schools and special gratitude to the TDIF Grant Committee in Fort Lauderdale, Florida, for all their support for this book.

Text copyright © 1995 by Rita Geller.
Illustrations copyright © 1997 by Rita Geller for pages 19 and 24.
Illustrations copyright © 1997 by Melissa Totten for cover, title page, pages 11, 21, 25, and 27.
Illustrations copyright © 1997 by Jennifer Payne for pages 2, 3, 23, and 32.
Illustrations copyright © 1997 by Sara Schuval for pages 5, 17, 28, and 31.
Illustrations copyright © 1997 by Ryan Kinsley, Jeremiah Fairthorne, and Michael Freedman for page 7.
Illustrations copyright © 1997 by Greg Pesicek for page 9.
Illustrations copyright © 1997 by Lindsay Hyde for pages 11, 15, and 29.
Illustrations copyright © 1997 by Rory Hickey for pages 9 and 13.

ISBN 0-439-31905-6

10 9 8 7 6 5 4 3 2 1
1 2 3 4 5/0

Printed in the U.S.A.   24
First Scholastic printing, May 1998

I met Sara, Ryan, Jeremiah, and Michelle.
We talked about the summer — there was
   so much to tell.

Some kids went camping. Some went
   on hikes.
Some told us about their new speed bikes.

Everyone was buzzing. There was chatter
   in the air.
Then some of the kids stopped and began
   to stare.

We saw one petite girl sitting — quiet
  and shy.
She smiled a funny smile. We noticed
  something unusual about her eye.

Her right eyelid drooped. Some of the
  students whispered and made fun.
She sat alone. She didn't seem to have
  many friends — maybe just one.

All our attention was directed her way.
She finally stood up and started to say,

"My name is Victoria. I have something
  to share."
We giggled, rolled our eyes, and really
  didn't care.

She sat down politely and without
  further delay,
we began our work. We were busy
  the rest of the day.

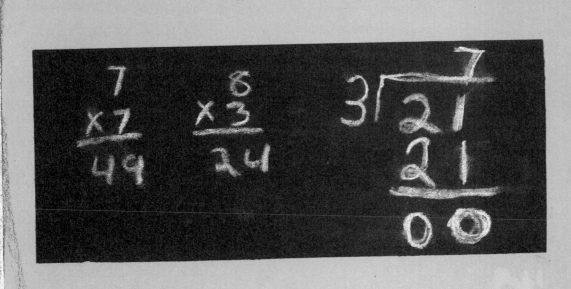

Weeks went by. Victoria didn't say much. She always did her work. She had an artist's touch.

One day our teacher said, "We are having a special guest.
You must listen carefully and behave your very best."

It was then that Victoria's mother
  began to speak.
The class was silent. Our curiosity
  was at a peak.

"Victoria," her mother clearly
  and slowly said,
"once had a cancerous tumor
  in her head."

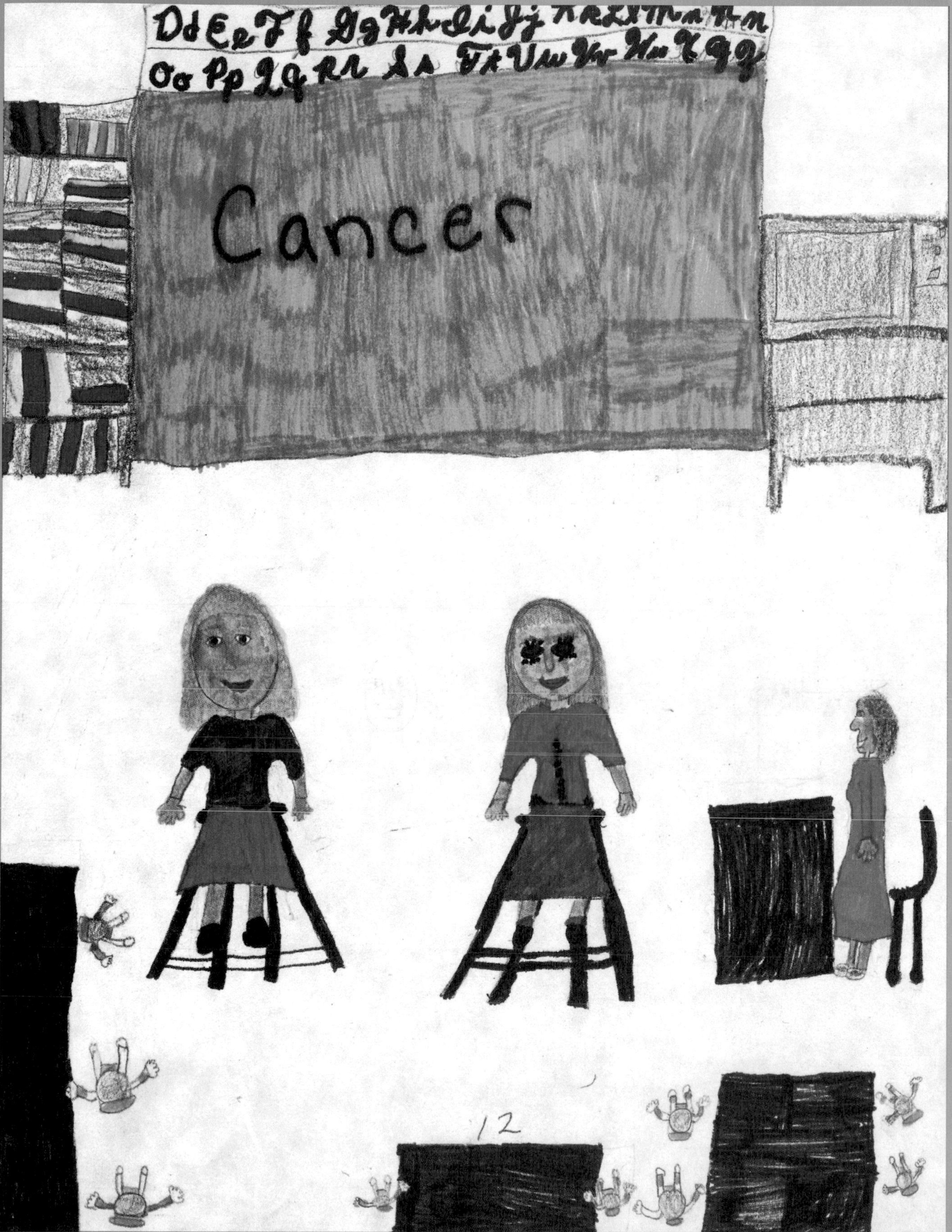
Cancer

We were shocked and overcome with fear!
Cancer? Our classmate? We listened with
a careful ear.

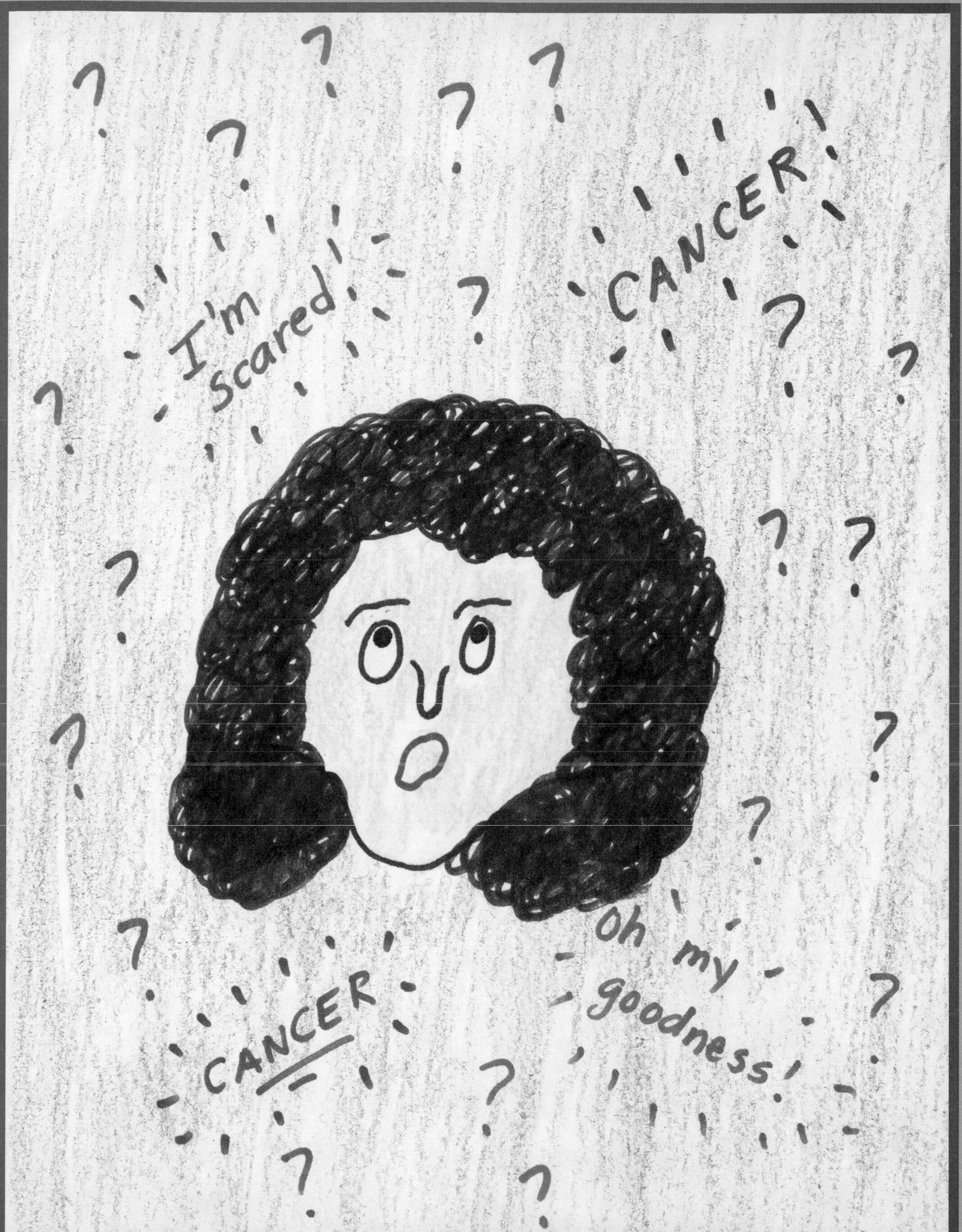
I'm Scared!
CANCER!
CANCER
Oh my goodness!

Her mother continued, "Victoria's tumor
    was near her right ear.
She had radiation and chemotherapy
    for more than a year.

"The weekly chemo made Victoria's hair
   fall out. That was a sight.
She had to wear a hat, but continued
   her cancer fight.

"The cancer killed the facial nerves
   on her right side.
And left her with a crooked smile
   that she cannot hide.

"There were lots of x-rays, medication,
   and days of pain.
But gradually her strength she began
   to regain.

"Classmates and family came to visit her at home. They wished her good cheer. Victoria received gifts, cards, and well-wishes throughout that whole year."

Her beautiful blonde hair has now grown back.
She's prettier than ever. That is a fact!

My class and I learned a lesson that should
  never be overlooked.
We learned that you cannot judge a person
  by the way he or she looks.

Victoria is courageous. She is brave, too.
She calmly talks about her cancer fight
  and what she's been through.

She has such a bright outlook on life;
  she's a miracle indeed.
Her positive attitude is something
  all people need.

We love to look at Victoria's special,
  sweet smile.
It reminds us never to give up—
  not even for a short while!

Never Give Up!!